# A Wise Monkey Tale

by
Betsy and
Giulio Maestro

Crown Publishers, Inc.
New York

Text copyright © 1975 by Betsy and Giulio Maestro
Illustrations copyright © 1975 by Giulio Maestro
All rights reserved. No part of this publication may be
reproduced, stored in a retrieval system, or transmitted, in any
form or by any means, electronic, mechanical, photocopying,
recording, or otherwise, without the prior written permission of
the publisher. Inquiries should be addressed to Crown Publishers, Inc.,
419 Park Avenue South, New York, N.Y. 10016.
Manufactured in the United States of America
Published simultaneously in Canada by General Publishing
Company Limited
Designed by Giulio Maestro
First Edition
The text of this book is set in 16 pt. Trump Medieval.
The illustrations are pen and ink wash paintings, executed
as four pre-separated halftones, printed in four colors.


Library of Congress Cataloging in Publication Data

Maestro, Betsy.
    A wise monkey tale.

    SUMMARY:  By using her wits, Monkey manages
literally to get herself out of a hole.
    [1.  Jungle stories]  I.  Maestro, Giulio, joint
author.  II.  Title.
PZ7.M267Wi            [E]              75-9749
ISBN 0-517-52328-0

A Wise Monkey Tale

One afternoon, Monkey was walking through the jungle eating a delicious banana cake wrapped in a banana leaf.

Monkey was so busy eating that she did not see
a large hole in the ground. Just as she took a big
juicy bite of her banana cake, she fell into the hole.

"Oh, dear!" thought Monkey. "How will I ever
get out of this hole?" She ate and she thought and
she thought and she ate. When she had finished
eating, she looked at the banana leaf.
"Aha!" said Monkey. "I have an idea!"

"Message from Gorilla! Message from Gorilla!"
shouted Monkey to the sky.
   "What's that you say?" came a deep voice from above.
Lion was prowling around the edge of the hole.
   "This is Gorilla's secret place," shouted Monkey,
"and he left a message written on this banana leaf.
   It says,
         " 'If very wise you wish to be
            Come down here, wait and see.' "

Lion looked down at Monkey and said, "Is that so!
Well, Gorilla is extremely wise, so I will take his
advice." And he bounded into the hole.

"What are you two doing down there?"
came another voice from above. Snake was
slithering around the edge of the hole.
   "Gorilla has left us an important message,"
roared Lion.
   "Yes, listen," and Monkey read,

   " 'If very wise you wish to be
      Come down here, wait and see.' "

"I would love to be very wise," hissed Snake. "May I join you?" And without waiting for an answer, Snake slid down into the hole.

Soon there was a new sound from above.
Zebra was grazing around the edge of the hole.
"Mind if I join the party?" she asked.

"We are not having a party! We are here to become as wise as Gorilla," said Lion.

"If you want to be very wise too, you may join us," added Monkey.

"Any reason is good enough for me," laughed Zebra, and she leaped into the hole.

"Why on earth are you all down in that hole?"
boomed Elephant, towering over the edge.
"We are all growing wise," said Snake.
"Read Elephant the banana leaf, Monkey," said Lion.
So Monkey read,
"'If very wise you wish to be
Come down here, wait and see.'"

"I am not at all sure that one becomes wise from sitting in a hole," said Elephant.

"But it says so quite clearly on Gorilla's banana leaf," replied Lion, "and you know that Gorilla is very, very smart."

"Well, that is true," said Elephant. "All right, make room for me." And she climbed into the hole.

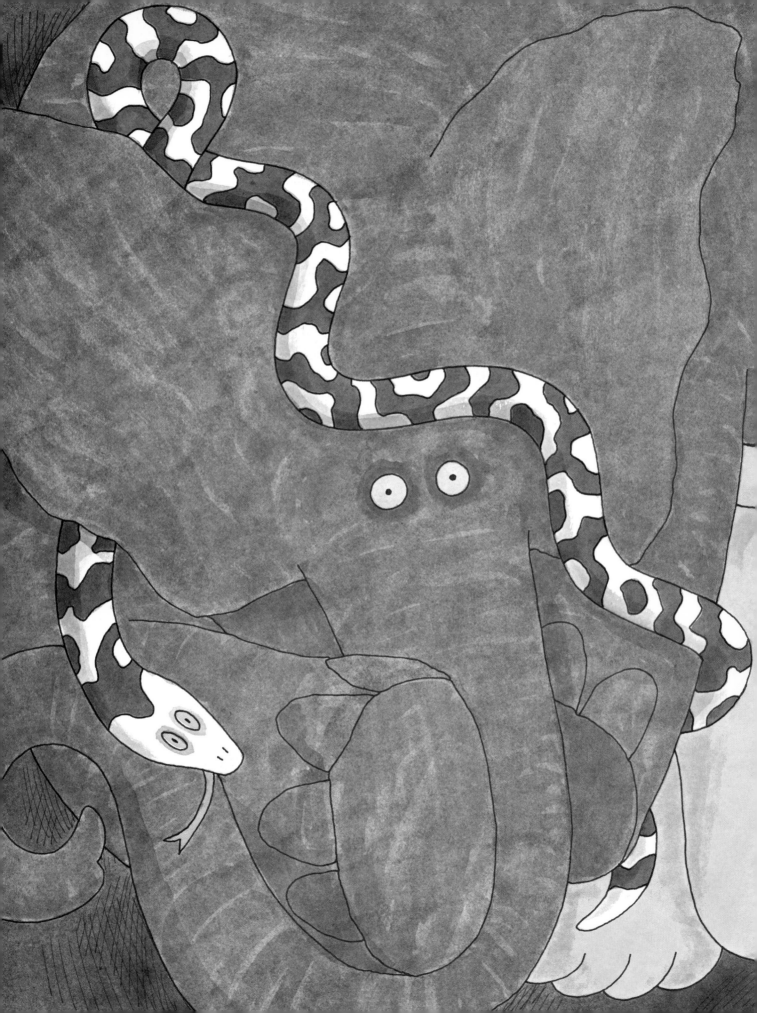

"I hope no one else comes along!" hissed Snake. "It is rather crowded in here," agreed Elephant.

"It certainly is," grumbled Lion. "We cannot fit anyone else in this hole."

"What should we do now, Monkey?" asked Zebra.

Monkey looked at everyone, and she looked at
the banana leaf in her hand. "Aha!" she said,
turning it over. "Here is another message.

" 'When fitting in another is in doubt
The first one in must climb out.' "

"Well, Monkey," said Snake, "you must leave first."
"You were the first one in," added Lion.
"Yes," agreed Zebra, "you must make room if
someone else comes along."

"Quite true," said Elephant. "Monkey has been here the longest, so she must leave first."
"Very well," replied Monkey, "then I might as well leave right now."

Quickly, Monkey climbed over the other animals
one by one to the very top of the hole.

"By the way, Monkey," shouted Lion, "was the banana leaf right? Are you wiser now than before?"

"You will all know very soon just how wise I am,"
said Monkey with a smile. And she grabbed hold of a
vine and swung up into a tree and disappeared.